A TOY MYSTEF

C000300187

THE **SEC**
CHATTER
BL◆CKS

Don Bosco

SUPER COOL BOOKS

First Printing, 2019

Printed by IngramSpark in the United States of America

ISBN 9789811417245

www.SuperCoolBooks.com

What we can imagine, we can create!

There are many ways

a story can unfold.

Pick your own path,

be *clever*,

be **bold**.

CONTENTS

ABOUT THIS GAMEBOOK

This is a work of fiction. Everything's made up. Just for fun.

This is also a gamebook. You choose what happens. There are a few different endings.

STORY

Kei and Will are students at the School of Amusement Arts in New Toy-ko City.

They help Professor Felicity Nora investigate unusual cases involving toys and puzzles.

A rare set of Chatter Blocks has been stolen. These Blocks talk when you roll them like dice.

Help Kei and Will catch the thief and recover the Blocks.

But be careful, the Perplexity Gang is involved!

WHO'S WHO

KEI: Fifth Year girl at the School of Amusement Arts (SAA). She's smart but often gets lost in her own thoughts. She daydreams too much!

WILL: Sixth Year boy at SAA. Works with Kei on the cases. He loves food and is often hungry.

PROFESSOR FELICITY NORA: Professor of Toy Criminology at SAA. She's determined to stop the Perplexity Gang. *(See below.)*

AGENT ANNA SWIFT: Works for the Odd Crimes Department of the International Toy Police (TOYPOL).

PERPLEXITY GANG: A small group of daring toy thieves. They can strike anywhere.

WELCOME TO NEW TOY-KO CITY

All the action takes place in the Third District of New Toy-ko City.

New Toy-ko City is the capital of the world's toy industry. Millions of dollars worth of toys and toy designs are bought and sold here every day.

The city was founded 150 years ago, just after the start of the Great Toy Revolution, which happened after the Universal Toy Declaration was signed by all the countries at the Assembly of All Nations. The countries pledged to use toy technologies to create a better world.

New Toy-Ko City is where you'll find all the best brains in toy tech.

And wealthy toy collectors.

And toy criminals too, who are always up to no good.

START HERE

[01]

DAY 1

9:34 A.M.

PLACE: SCHOOL OF AMUSEMENT ARTS.

This morning's class is Toy History, taught by Mr. Nogambe.

Kei is fascinated.

Mr. Nogambe is talking about shadow puppets.

His voice is so deep, the first time that Kei heard him speak, she couldn't help thinking of a gigantic elephant snoring gently in the shade.

"Shadow puppets are one of the oldest toys in the world," Mr. Nogambe says. "Children twisted twigs into animal shapes, and held these in front of

5

a fire, to create moving shadows. Can you imagine the fantastic creatures that appeared on their cave walls?"

Kei is already busy, making up these images in her head, as she pictures the shadow animals.

Kei has about twenty questions, and she can't decide which one to ask first. Just as she decides to put up her hand, she sees Will standing outside the classroom door.

He's hopping up and down in excitement, and his face says he has something important to tell her.

Will pulls out his phone and holds it up for Kei to see before texting a message.

BZZZZZZZZZZ. Kei's phone jumps in her pocket. She quickly reads Will's message: "Professor has a big case for us!"

★ **How thrilling! Go see Professor Nora first thing after class.**
[FLIP TO PAGE 7]

[02]

DAY 1
10:12 A.M.

Kei and Will are in Professor Nora's office. There are lots of unusual toys everywhere, and stacks of books and files about the Perplexity Gang.

Professor Nora says, "Mr. Richard Beetle is a famous toy collector. You've probably heard of his online store, Rich Beetle Toy Emporium?"

Kei and Will nod.

"Well, someone stole his Chatter Blocks," Professor Nora says. "He's asked us to help him get them back."

Will is puzzled. "Uh, Chatter Blocks?"

Kei's writing all this down. Her pen flies furiously across the notebook page.

"What are those?" Kei asks.

"No idea," Professor Nora admits. "Go see Mr. Beetle and find out what they are, and what's going on. Can I trust you two with this case?"

★ Yes, go see Mr. Beetle right away.
[FLIP TO PAGE 17]

★ Why not interview Mr. Beetle's neighbors first? They might know something.
[FLIP TO PAGE 24]

DAY 2
9:45 A.M.

The next morning.

Kei is waiting for Will outside the school library. She can't wait to tell him the story she came across in an old journal:

A thousand years ago, there was a widow who found some Chatter Blocks in her husband's old chests. She hid them under her bed, and would stay up late at night rolling them over and over again. She didn't know about the bells inside. She just loved how they talked to her. Soon she refused to have anything to do with normal life. She spent her days and nights in the room, rolling the Chatter Blocks over and over again. Sometimes they made her laugh. Sometimes she would scold them. Sometimes she would hug them and cry. She didn't wash, eat, change her clothes, go out, clean the house, or meet with anyone. Her young son was left to look after himself. He ran away from home and joined the army. Years passed. One day he became the Governor of the district. His mother had passed on. But he remembered how those Chatter Blocks had ruined his childhood. And so he passed a law. Toys were banned. Anyone caught playing with them would be locked up. Anyone caught selling them or passing them around would be executed. From that day, nobody dared to touch a toy. Thus began the Dark Ages of Toy History, one thousand years ago.

Will is late. When he finally appears, he has a streak of chocolate cream across his left cheek.

No prizes for guessing what he had been busy with just before this.

"I can't help liking Mr. Hiro," Kei says. "There's something nice about him. But we do have to investigate every suspect thoroughly."

They go to the school's computer room and search the internet for information about Mr. Hiro.

"Looks like he travels a lot for work," Will says. "This year alone he's performed in Japan, parts of China, Australia, Mexico, and Canada."

Kei's phone beeps. The screen shows the caller's name.

"It's Professor Nora," Kei tells Will.

They hurry out of the computer room, and Kei hits the speaker button on her phone so Will can hear too.

"I just heard from a contact at TOYPOL," Professor Nora says, sounding rather unhappy.

"Hieronymus Hiro left town last night. He also paid his landlord the last month's rent, and said he's moving away for good."

Will's jaw drops. "He's run away with the Blocks. I knew it. He was up to no good."

★ "Back to lessons then, two of you," Professor Nora says.

END

★ They were close to solving this! Explore another ending.

[FLIP TO PAGE 7]

[04]

DAY 1
12:55 PM

Kei and Will return to school. They look for Professor Nora.

"Mr. Beetle says Madam Polly Blavs turned up while he was out," Kei reports. "She broke the back window so she could get in."

Professor Nora frowns. "Madam Blavs is the wife of a foreign prince. She could easily buy her own Blocks. Why steal them?"

Will shrugs.

"Mr. Beetle had two other guests yesterday," Kei says. "Mr. Simonington Chu, who owns an artificial intelligence software company, and Mr. Hieronymus Hiro, an actor. They met to discuss outing plans for the local Historical Hobbies Club. They're the committee members."

"The three of them are our suspects for now," Professor Nora says. "Start interviewing them, and see if there's anything suspicious."

★ Go back and question neighbors.
[FLIP TO PAGE 21]

★ Visit the suspects and start interviewing them.
[FLIP TO PAGE 27]

DAY 2
9:53 AM

Madam Blavs lives on Second Street, in a beautiful penthouse overlooking Middle Park.

She has servants running all around, cleaning the vases and fluffing the cushions.

Her two big dogs snarl at Kei and Will, but Madam Blavs scolds them and then they start whimpering like helpless little babies.

Kei asks about the handbag incident that Hieronymus Hiro brought up.

"An honest mistake," Madame Blavs retorts. "I own the same handbag. Seventeen of them, in fact. They're in my other apartment, in the First District."

"Uh, what happened at Mr. Beetle's house yesterday?" Will asks. "Could you tell us your version?"

"I knocked repeatedly," Madam Blavs says.

"Then I walked to the back of the house. The path was all muddy. Tripped over a brick and broke my heel. How annoying! I saw that the glass pane above the door handle was broken, so I reached inside carefully and let myself in."

Madam Blavs pauses for a moment before continuing,

"Simonington was in the dining room. I called my driver to get a pair of shoes from home. Simonington kept making angry faces at me. What a rude man."

Madam Blavs sneers.

"Anyway, I have my own Chatter Blocks," she says. "Gold plated. With diamonds. And a Certificate of Authenticity. I would never steal Richard Beetle's miserable set."

★ Mr Beetle might need investigating.
[FLIP TO PAGE 35]

★ Surely Mr Beetle's neighbors saw someone suspicious?
[FLIP TO PAGE 38]

[06]

DAY 1
11:32 AM

In Mr. Beetle's basement study.

He has a curly mustache. Light blue shirt. Purple suspenders.

And a strange cough too.

It sounds like this, "**KRRF!** **KRRF.**"

"While I was out yesterday afternoon," he says, "the thief broke a glass pane and unlocked the back door. Then she came downstairs and stole my Chatter Blocks."

"What are Chatter Blocks, sir?" Will asks. He's dying to know. Kei too.

"Six-sided blocks," he says, "about two inches high, with tiny bells inside. Invented in Egypt ages ago. Very rare these days."

Mr Beetle shows them a video about the Blocks.

"Each bell produces a syllable," the video explains. "Like HUH or **GOR** or **DUH** or ʃoH. When the Blocks are rolled, like dice, the bells inside get knocked around. You hear a string of syllables, like a spoken phrase or sentence. Sometimes it's nonsense, but sometimes you actually make out the words. It can give very profound advice."

Kei and Will exchange glances. What a fantastic toy!

Kei tries to imagine the things it might say to her.

Will recalls that Mr. Beetle had said "she" when referring to the thief.

He asks, "Sir, do you suspect anyone in particular?"

Without hesitating, Mr. Beetle roars, "Madam Polly Blavs!"

★ Return to school and tell Professor Nora.
[FLIP TO PAGE 13]

★ Question the neighbors.
[FLIP TO PAGE 21]

[07]

DAY 2
2:46 PM

Kei and Will sit in Professor Nora's office.
Professor Nora gets off the phone.

"Mr. Beetle just confirmed that he has five sisters but no brother," Professor Nora says to them. "Now tell me what else you've learned."

Kei opens her notebook. "Mr. Chu and Mr. Beetle are old friends. Mr. Chu claims he wouldn't steal the Blocks from Mr. Beetle. But he was waiting by himself in the house. He would have had a chance to do it."

Will chips in, "Mr Hiro arrived last. He wouldn't have had the chance to steal the Blocks. He says Madam Blavs probably took them. Mr. Beetle thinks so too."

"Did that boy see anything else?" Professor Nora asks.

"I'm not sure we can trust him," Will says. "He could have made up that story about Mr. Beetle's brother just to be naughty."

Professor Nora leans back and thinks.

"Hmm . . . Mr. Beetle also checked with his housekeeper," Professor Nora says. "She insists nobody else visited, aside from these three Historical Hobbies Club members. She's still furious. She said all three came in with muddy shoes, right after she had cleaned the floor."

Kei raises her eyebrows.

"Let's confirm that with Mrs. Hughes again," she says. "And then we should get Agent Anna's help."

★ Has Kei cracked the case? Consult Agent Anna Swift.
[FLIP TO PAGE 47]

★ Kei knows who did it! No time to lose. Confront the suspect right away.
[FLIP TO PAGE 40]

DAY 1
1:15 PM

Kei and Will go looking for neighbors to interview. They walk around and knock on doors. Nobody wants to talk to them.

"This investigating work is tiring," Will announces. "Let's go get some lunch, and we can discuss the case there."

They find a cafe, and order their food. The music is very loud.

Kei pulls out her phone and searches for information about the Chatter Blocks.

Here's what she finds:

Four thousand years ago, somewhere in the East, there was a King who had seven daughters and he loved his youngest one most of all. He asked his Royal Inventors to capture his voice in an instrument, so that his daughter could always hear him talking to her, even after his death. The Royal Inventors worked for many years. Finally they came up with these Chatter Blocks. The bells inside were crafted to match the King's voice. And so the King's wish was fulfilled. After the King died, whenever someone wanted to get his advice, they would ask his daughter to roll the Blocks so they could hear what he had to say.

Kei is astonished. She's about to share this with Will, when suddenly:

BEEPY-BEEP!

Kei has an incoming call.

She takes out her phone. It's Professor Nora.

"Where are you?" Professor Nora says.

Kei gives a quick report. She almost has to shout, because of the music.

Professor Nora sighs. "I expected you to get a lot more done by now. Instead, it sounds like you're at some sort of party. Never mind, come back to school and carry on with your lessons. I'll take over from here."

Kei tells Will. He looks glum.

"Bummer!" he says, as he stuffs more fries into his mouth. "I was hoping we'd get to stay out all day."

END

★ Let's go back to the start and find another ending!
[FLIP TO PAGE 7]

[09]

DAY 1
11:45 AM

Kei and Will walk around the neighborhood. They look out for clues.

A boy rides his unicycle past them. He shows off a few stunts, like spinning his unicycle around and cycling backwards in a circle.

There's no one else around, but Kei has an uncomfortable feeling, like there's someone watching them.

"Seems like a peaceful street," Kei says. "Nothing suspicious here. Let's go see Mr. Beetle, shall we?"

Suddenly Will grabs her arm and points to a house across the street.

"That woman in the window!" Will says. "If she

was looking out like this yesterday, she might have spotted something."

Will runs over toward the house before Kei can stop him.

Ten minutes later, Kei and Will are seated in the woman's kitchen.

She serves them chocolate milk and her special chocolate chip cookies.

"My son's favorite!" she says. "I can always make him a new batch."

The woman introduces herself as Mrs. Silva.

The day before, she had seen Mr. Beetle go out, come back, go out again in a hurry, and return two hours later.

While he was away, a woman and a man came to see him. But the housekeeper was busy, so they went around the back.

Kei thinks the cookies taste horrible. Will finishes them anyway.

★ Kei and Will go to talk to more neighbors.
[FLIP TO PAGE 21]

★ Stay and ask more questions about what Mrs. Silva saw.
[FLIP TO PAGE 31]

DAY 1
2:17 PM

Kei and Will take the bus.

The east side of Southend Road is a beautiful neighborhood, with rows of elegant buildings.

"Professor said to start with Hieronymus Hiro," Kei says to Will. "But why?"

Will shrugs. "I'm hungry. Let's go eat after this."

When they get to Hieronymus Hiro's apartment, he opens the door.

"I'm busy packing," he says apologetically. "Leaving tomorrow to star in a movie, you see."

His living room is kind of creepy because there's a tall black marble statue of an angry ape in the corner.

"What happened yesterday?" Kei asks.

"I arrived last," Hiro recalls. "Mrs. Hughes, Mr. Beetle's housekeeper, let me in. I joined the meeting and we discussed our annual outing. Lots of disagreement, as always. Nothing was confirmed."

"Were any of the other members acting suspiciously?" Will asks. "Could they have taken the Blocks?"

"Well, Madam Blavs once went off with another member's expensive handbag," Hiro says. "She has this nasty habit."

★ Something suspicious about Madam Blavs!
[FLIP TO PAGE 29]

★ Interview Simonington Chu next.
[FLIP TO PAGE 33]

〔 11 〕

DAY 1
5:27 PM

Kei and Will leave Hieronymus Hiro's apartment. Will is hungry, as usual. They spot a hot dog stand outside the park, down the road.

Will gets a hot dog with everything on it.

Kei gets a small bag of churros.

They find a seat in the park and eat.

"What do you think about what Mr. Hiro said?" Will asks with his mouth full.

A speck of his half-chewed bun flies out of his mouth and almost lands on Kei's arm, but she dodges it in time.

"Mr. Beetle had the same opinion," Kei says. "He blamed Madam Blavs, although he had no proof."

"No smoke without fire, that's what they say,"

Will replies. "They must have good reasons not to trust her."

Kei chews slowly. Her brain is spinning like a mad engine, trying to piece all the information together.

"Or one of them could be sending us on a wild goose chase," Kei says. "Maybe they have something to hide."

Will nods. That's worth considering.

★ Investigate Hieronymus Hiro!
[FLIP TO PAGE 9]

★ Investigate Richard Beetle!
[FLIP TO PAGE 35]

DAY 1
12:30 PM

Mrs. Silva's son comes home. He's dressed in a suit and he carries a slim briefcase.

He's not a child. He looks like he might be fifty years old.

He probably does something very serious for a living. He could be a famous politician, just that Kei and Will don't recognize him.

The son does not introduce himself when he comes in. Instead he first notices the crumbs on the cookie tray. Not a single one of his favorite cookies was left for him.

He glares at Kei and Will.

"Who are you?" he wants to know. "What are you doing in my house?"

He's used to shouting at people.

Mrs. Silva says, "Oh, they just want to ask some questions about our neighbor."

Will tries to explain. "Our teacher is investigating--**OW**!"

He stops suddenly because Kei kicked him under the table. She shoots him an angry look, then smiles sweetly at her host. "We're doing a research project about this neighborhood, sir. It's for our school, extra credit you know."

Mrs. Silva's son isn't impressed.

"Which school would that be?" he wants to know. He glances at the cookie tray again. "I will call the principal up right now and complain. Don't ever show your faces around here again. Or you'll regret it!"

He means what he says.

Kei feels a shudder run down her spine.

END

★ At least Will enjoyed his cookies! Look for another ending?
[FLIP TO PAGE 7]

DAY 1
5:02 PM

Next, Kei and Will go to Simonington Chu's office on Roundabout Road, where the big banks and office buildings are located.

His artificial intelligence company is called Skull & Software.

The left side of his mouth twitches now and then. But he never actually smiles.

"No one answered the front door when I got there," he remembers, "so I went around the back and shouted. Got my shoes all muddy! Mrs Hughes, the housekeeper, finally heard me. She had been vacuuming on the third floor; that's why she didn't hear me ring the doorbell. She popped her head out of a window and said she'd open the front door for me. So I went back to the front."

He said he then waited in the dining room for Rich to get back.

"Madam Blavs arrived next," Simonington Chu says. "She acted suspiciously, and she used her phone a lot."

As Kei and Will are leaving, Chu tells them, "Richard Beetle is my childhood buddy. I invested in his toy business. I'd never steal anything from him. But I don't trust that Hiro."

★ Interview Madam Blavs next.
[FLIP TO PAGE 15]

★ Hieronymus Hiro's story needs looking into!
[FLIP TO PAGE 9]

[14]

DAY 2
12:02 PM

Kei has to attend a lecture on Clockwork Toys before lunch break.

But right when the bell rings after the session, she runs to the canteen, and finds Will sitting next to the drinks counter.

He has just started on a banana milk shake.

"Did you find anything?" Kei asks.

Will was supposed to use Professor Nora's computer to access the TOYPOL website to see if Richard Beetle had any links to criminals.

Will takes his time slurping up the last of his milk shake.

"Ah!" he grunts in satisfaction, before telling Kei about his discovery.

"Mr Beetle used to own a toy factory," he says, "but not in this city. The factory was shut down years ago because it was making illegal copies of popular toys and selling them as the real thing."

Kei's eyes grow wide.

"He's a toy pirate?" she says.

Will shrugs. "The other partners were arrested. But Mr. Beetle insisted that he was never really involved with the factory. He just loaned them money to start the business. TOYPOL couldn't find much evidence against him, so they let him go in the end."

Professor Nora suddenly appears, waving an empty tin of biscuits. She looks mad enough to hit someone with the empty tin.

"There you are!" she says to Will. "I let you use my computer. I didn't say you could help yourself to my Danish biscuits. My sister just sent these to me, and I haven't even had one. I was planning to have some for tea today."

"Uh-oh," Will says. "I'm so sorry, Professor Nora."

And then, with all that banana milk shake inside him, he burps loudly.

"uuuuuuuuuRRRRRRRRPPPP!"

His face turns red with embarrassment because the other students have turned around to stare at him. Many are laughing and making rude faces.

Professor Nora stares into her empty biscuit tin, before looking at Will again. "I should have known better than to ask for your help," she says. "From now on, you're off the case. I'll find the Chatter Blocks thief myself."

END

★ Start over and this time help Kei and Will find the thief.
[FLIP TO PAGE 7]

[15]

DAY 2
12:24 PM

Kei and Will are back in Mr. Beetle's neighborhood. Will spots a boy on a unicycle coming down the street. He's riding it very confidently. Looks like he lives around here.

Will walks over to chat.

"Noticed anyone suspicious here?" Will asks the boy.

"Just you two," the boy sniggers. "Are you detectives?"

"No," Kei says. "We're helping a toy criminologist."

The boy's disappointed.

"Well, Mr. Beetle's brother visited yesterday," he says. "First time seeing him."

"Eh?" Will says.

Kei starts recording the conversation on her phone.

The boy nods. "Same clothes, same cough, same way of walking. I thought it was Mr. Beetle, but when I waved to him, he didn't wave back as he normally would. That's when I noticed this man was a bit smaller than Mr. Beetle."

According to the boy, the mysterious brother visited when Mr. Beetle was out. He didn't stay long.

As they thank the boy and walk off, Kei asks Will, "Why didn't Mr. Beetle mention his brother?"

★ Return to school and review clues.
[FLIP TO PAGE 19]

★ Confront Mr Beetle about his brother.
[FLIP TO PAGE 44]

DAY 2
4:22 PM

Professor Nora arranges for Agent Anna to meet them across the street from Hieronymus Hiro's apartment.

They hurry down, but there's no sign of Agent Anna.

Kei explains how she realized that all their clues point to Hieronymus Hiro.

"Mr. Beetle's housekeeper says all three Historical Hobbies Club members entered with muddy shoes," Kei says. "From what the boy on the unicycle told us, the thief very likely came early, disguised as Mr. Beetle. He broke in through the back, took the Chatter Blocks and left. When Mr. Hiro turned up for the meeting, his shoes were muddy too. That would only be possible if he had gone round the back, like the others did. Which he didn't need to. My hunch is that he had disguised himself as Mr. Beetle, then broken in just after the real Mr. Beetle had left. He would have fooled all the neighbors, except for that eagle-eyed boy. And also, Mr Hiro forgot to clean his shoes before going back as himself."

That was a lot of explaining! Kei was almost out of breath when she was done.

Professor Nora nods. "Good deduction. We'll find out for sure when Agent Anna turns up. She'll also have a warrant to search his apartment."

"Hey, that's Mr Hiro!" Will suddenly says. He points across the street. "We have to stop him."

Hieronymus Hiro is walking quickly towards a waiting taxi.

They run over to him.

"Stop, Mr. Hiro!" Professor Nora says.

Mr. Hiro looks over his shoulder, with a flicker of

panic on his face. But just as quickly he changes his expression.

"Why?" he asks calmly.

"We have something urgent to discuss with you, sir," Kei says.

Mr. Hiro stares at them for a while. Then he smiles politely.

"Sure, let's go upstairs then," he says. "I'll need to be off soon, though."

The four of them get into the elevator.

Mr Hiro presses the button.

The elevator goes up.

PING! It stops on Mr Hiro's floor.

"This way," he says.

He takes them to his apartment.

He unlocks the door.

But then he fumbles and drops his keycard.

"After you," he says to Professor Nora, as he bends down to pick it up.

Professor Nora nods. She goes in.

Kei and Will follow her.

"Make yourselves at home," Mr. Hiro says. "Don't be shy."

Then, while still outside the apartment door, he quickly pulls it shut.

TEE—TEE—TEEET!

Mr. Hiro has activated the electronic lock!

"He's locked us in," Professor Nora says in horror as she tries to open the door. "And by the time we get out, he could be far away."

Kei looks glum. They were so close.

"Well," she says. "At least we now know that my hunch is correct."

END

★ Mystery solved! Start over and explore other endings?

[FLIP TO PAGE 7]

[17]

DAY 2
2:13 PM

Kei and Will walk over and ring Mr. Beetle's doorbell.

"I think his brother stole Mr. Beetle's Chatter Blocks," Will says excitedly. "That's our case solved. We're brilliant, aren't we? All it took was some asking around. Don't forget, I was the one who approached this boy."

Mrs. Hughes the housekeeper answers.

"Mr Beetle is busy," she says. "You can wait in the dining room until he's ready."

Twenty minutes later, Mr. Beetle enters.

He looks surprised.

"Have you found my Chatter Blocks so quickly?" he says. "Madam Blavs stole them, didn't she?"

Kei's heart is beating hard. She's nervous.

"Sir, we're been talking with one of the neighborhood kids," Kei says. "He actually saw the thief."

She's about to continue, when Will shouts,

"Your brother is the thief! He stole your Chatter Blocks!"

Mr. Beetle pulls back in surprise.

His eyebrows shoot so high up, they look like they will jump off his face.

"You two are quite crazy," he says. He takes a deep breath to calm himself. "Firstly, I have a few sisters. But I don't have a brother. So he couldn't have stolen the Chatter Blocks. Secondly, you were supposed to investigate the members of the Historical Hobbies Club who were here yesterday. Not go gossiping with the bratty kids that live on this street."

Oops.

Will regrets his outburst.

And Kei feels her heart drop like a stone.

It was a bad idea after all, approaching Mr. Beetle like this.

Mr. Beetle glares at them. "Get. Out. Of. My. House!"

Kei and Will go back to school.

They head straight for Professor Nora's office.

"Mr. Beetle just called me to complain," she says sternly. "Looks like it wasn't such a good idea to send you two."

END

★ Good job getting this far! You can start over and explore other endings.

[FLIP TO PAGE 7]

[18]

DAY 2
4:18 PM

WHERE: Agent Anna Swift's office, at the TOYPOL Building.

PEOPLE PRESENT: Professor Nora. Kei and Will.
Richard Beetle.

Hieronymus Hiro, Simonington Chu and Madame Polly Blavs.

Plus Agent Anna herself.

"**KRRF! KRRF.**" Mr. Beetle coughs.

"Now that everyone is here, we can begin," Agent Anna says.

"Make this quick," Mr. Hiro grumbles. "I've a train to catch."

Professor Nora stands in the middle. She gives them a short version of what Kei and Will found out.

"Did that boy make up his story?" she says. "Maybe not. Perhaps the thief came early, disguised as Mr. Beetle. Even with the cough. The thief broke in through the back, took the Chatter Blocks, and walked off with them before anyone else arrived."

Mr. Beetle gasps. "The audacity!"

Madam Blavs laughs. "Ha! How easy! It couldn't have been me, then. I wouldn't pass off as Mr. Beetle's brother. Not in a thousand years."

Mr. Chu looks upset. "Surely you don't think it was me," he says.

Kei stands up. "Mr. Hiro said he was the last to arrive," she says. "But what if he was also the first?"

All turn to look at Mr. Hiro now.

"Mr. Hiro, you told us Mrs. Hughes let you in when you arrived," Will says. "But she's certain about your muddy shoes. It would only be muddy if you had gone round the back earlier, like the others did. But you didn't need to. You turned up much later. After Mrs. Hughes was done with her vacuuming."

Mr. Hiro sits up straight. "What are you getting at?"

"You're an actor," Professor Nora says. "You impersonate people for a living. You came very early. Disguised as Mr. Beetle. But that boy on the unicycle wasn't fooled, you see."

Mr. Hiro takes a deep breath. His expression remains calm, but his neck is turning red.

Agent Anna goes to stand at the door. In case Mr. Hiro tries to run out.

"Perhaps you'd let us search your bags, Mr. Hiro," Agent Anna says. She looks stern. "And your apartment. If you have nothing to hide."

Mr. Hiro sighed.

"Indeed, I took the Blocks," he admitted. "But trust me, the horrible heartless villain here is Richard Beetle."

★ What's going on? Let's find out!
[FLIP TO PAGE 50]

DAY 3
10:42 AM

NEXT MORNING. IN THE SCHOOL CANTEEN.

Professor Nora is treating Kei and Will to some delicious chicken pie. Still warm from the oven.

"I wasn't expecting it to end like that," Professor Nora admitted.

Will scratches his head.

"Let's see if I got it right," he says. "The Perplexity Gang stole the Chatter Blocks sent from a small village museum in Mexico. The Gang then offered the Blocks to Richard Beetle. He knew, but he bought them anyway. That's why he hired Professor Nora, instead of reporting the theft to the police."

"The villagers collect money from tourists who come to see the Blocks," Kei says. "Without the Blocks, the villagers have no income."

"But Mr. Hiro somehow found out the truth," Professor Nora says. "He decided to steal the Blocks and send them back to the villagers. He should have just informed TOYPOL, but he thought they might not make this case a priority."

Kei looks concerned. "Will Mr. Hiro go to prison?"

Professor Nora says, "I'll check with Agent Anna and let you know. It's a complicated situation. Both Mr. Beetle and Mr. Hiro are now assisting Agent Anna with her investigation. Hopefully, they'll help her catch the leaders of the Perplexity Gang."

"Yum!" Will says. He eagerly pops the last bit of chicken pie into his mouth and licks his fingers.

Kei laughs. "Have you been listening at all, Will?"

Professor Nora beams at them. "Never mind. You two are excellent toy investigators. Great work!"

They go back to Professor Nora's office, where she has the set of Chatter Blocks. Agent Anna had asked her to examine them and verify that they are the real thing. And indeed they are.

Kei and Will spend the rest of that day playing with the Blocks. They roll the Blocks over and over again. There are only bells inside. But still the Blocks seem to answer their questions, make them laugh, and tease them.

What marvelous ingenuity it must have taken to create these lovely toys, such a long time ago.

END

★ Start over and find other endings?
[FLIP TO PAGE 7]

★ Or read about how we made this gamebook!
[FLIP TO PAGE 53]

CREDITS

This gamebook was created with these tools: notebook and pen, Twine software, Scrivener, LibreOffice.

You can use Twine to make your own story gamebook too! Give it a try.

❖

THE AUTHOR:

Don Bosco writes fun stories for young readers. He lives in Singapore.

Website: http://www.SuperCoolBooks.com

Email: studio@SuperCoolBooks.com

❖

MORE CREDITS:

Illustrations by Mark Bosco.

Playtesting by Luke Bosco.

Cover design and book layout by Christabel Chew.

Lightning Source UK Ltd.
Milton Keynes UK
UKHW010648100822
407113UK00003B/1159